P9-DGQ-007

Remember That

BY LESLÉA NEWMAN

ILLUSTRATED BY KAREN RITZ

Clarion Books
New York

Clarion Books
a Houghton Mifflin Company imprint
215 Park Avenue South, New York, NY 10003
Original text copyright © 1993 by *Highlights for Children*
New material copyright © 1996
by Lesléa Newman
Illustrations copyright © 1996 by Karen Ritz

Illustrations executed in watercolor.
Type is 16/20-point Sabon.

Library of Congress Cataloging-in-Publication Data
Newman, Lesléa.
Remember that / by Lesléa Newman ; illustrated by Karen Ritz.
p. cm.
Summary: Though Grandmother ages, she still has important lessons to teach
about life as she asks her granddaughter to "Remember that."
ISBN 0-395-66589-2
[1. Grandmothers—Fiction. 2. Old age—Fiction.] I. Ritz, Karen, ill. II. Title.
PZ7.N47988Re 1995
[E]—dc20   94-27874
CIP
AC

TWP   10 9 8 7 6 5 4 3 2 1

FOR MY GRANDMOTHER, RUTH LEVIN
may her memory be a blessing
L.N.

FOR MY GRANDMOTHER RITZ
K.R.

Friday is my favorite night of the week because Friday
night is *Shabbos*, and *Shabbos* is my special time with
Bubbe.

Before it gets dark, I run across the street to Bubbe's
apartment.

"*Shabbat shalom, shayneh maideleh*," Bubbe says.
That means, "Good Sabbath, beautiful girl." Then Bubbe
kisses my face and leaves red lipstick on my cheek that
I wipe off with the back of my hand.

Bubbe's house is sparkling clean. I help her set the table. Before I put the silverware out, I rub each piece with a cloth so it shines.

Bubbe nods, pleased. "Everyone who wants to eat has to help out a little. Remember that."

Then she lights the two white candles in her shiny candlesticks. We both make three circles with our hands to gather in the *Shabbos* light, and we say the special *Shabbos* prayer together before we sit down to eat.

"Always eat when you're hungry. Remember that," Bubbe says.

I laugh. "Bubbe, it would be silly to eat if I wasn't hungry," I say.

Bubbe puts a bowl of soup down in front of me and says, "*Ess a bissl*." That means eat a little, but I eat a lot because Bubbe makes the best chicken soup in the whole wide world. In fact, even if I wasn't hungry, I would probably eat this big bowl anyway! Bubbe's soup has carrots and celery and onions and potatoes in it. The chicken is sweet as honey, and the matzo balls are nice and chewy. I always eat three.

Now I am a little older, and Bubbe doesn't feel so good. Her legs hurt, and she has to sit down most of the time. It's a good thing I'm getting taller, so I can reach our soup bowls when Bubbe is too tired to get out of her chair.

"Always rest when you're tired," Bubbe says. "Remember that."

"I'll remember," I tell Bubbe.

Bubbe is too tired to clean her house anymore, and she's too tired to cook, so now she's coming to live with us.

Bubbe moves in on a Friday.

"C'mon, Bubbe," I say. "We have to make the chicken soup."

"Let Bubbe lie down and rest," Mama says.

"But what about the soup?" I ask.

"I'll make it," Mama says. "I know how."

Even though Mama's soup has carrots and celery and onions and potatoes in it, it isn't the same. The chicken isn't very sweet, and the matzo balls crumble. I eat two, to be polite. Then I take a bowl of soup in to Bubbe.

"*Shabbat shalom, shayneh maideleh*," Bubbe says.

"Are you sick, Bubbe?" I ask.

"No, *shayneh maideleh*, I'm just tired."

"Always rest when you're tired," I remind Bubbe. "Remember that."

I like having Bubbe live at our house. I get to see her every day, not just on *Shabbos*. Sometimes I bring Bubbe breakfast in bed. Sometimes I play cards with her after school. She teaches me to play knock-rummy, and I teach her how to play crazy-eights.

Now I'm even older, and Bubbe is sick. She can't walk at all, and we have to take her to a nursing home.

I cry the day Bubbe moves away.

"I'm going to miss you, Bubbe," I say.

Mama cries too, but Bubbe doesn't cry at all.

"I'll miss you too, but you have to go wherever life sends you," Bubbe says. "Remember that. When I had to leave Russia to come to America, I made the best of it. I'll make the best of this too, *shayneh maideleh*. And you can come visit me on *Shabbos*."

I go visit Bubbe at her nursing home the very next *Shabbos*. I bring her a big bouquet of daisies and daffodils, her two most favorite flowers.

There are lots of people in the lobby at the nursing home, but I see Bubbe right away. She's sitting in a wheelchair, waiting for me, with her pocketbook on her lap.

"*Shabbat shalom, shayneh maideleh*," Bubbe says.

"*Shabbat shalom*, Bubbe," I answer.

I bend down to give Bubbe a hug, and I feel a little funny because Bubbe's the one who always bends down to hug me. I've never seen her in a wheelchair before. I ask her if she likes it.

"It's very good. It helps me rest my legs," Bubbe says. "Come, let's go into the dining room for supper."

I wheel Bubbe into the dining room and sit down next to her at a table. A woman in a yellow uniform serves us chicken soup. I taste it, but it isn't nearly as good as Bubbe's. It isn't even as good as Mama's.

"This chicken is tough," I say to Bubbe. "And look, there's rice in the soup. There isn't even one matzo ball."

"*Shah*," Bubbe says, holding one finger up to her lips. "Not everyone has enough to eat in this world. Always be grateful that you have food on your plate. Remember that, and add a *bissl* salt."

I shake some salt into my soup and it tastes a little better, but still, I only eat a few spoonfuls.

After supper we take the elevator up to the second floor, and Bubbe shows me her room. She has a bed, a dresser, a closet, a telephone, a TV, and a big picture of me hanging on her wall. I put the flowers I brought in a vase and put it on Bubbe's dresser.

"It's crowded in here," I say to Bubbe. Her room is much smaller than her old apartment. It's even smaller than my room at home.

"*Shah*," Bubbe says, raising her finger again. "Some people have no place to live at all. Always be grateful you have a roof over your head. Remember that."

Bubbe takes me to the second-floor lounge. "This is Mrs. Sullivan. We play cards together," Bubbe says.

"How do you do?" Mrs. Sullivan says. "Your grandmother is a very good card player. She taught me how to play crazy-eights."

"Bubbe, I taught you that," I say, and Bubbe smiles.

"This is Mr. Velez. He fixed my television for me," Bubbe says.

"How do you do?" Mr. Velez says. "You know, you look just like your grandma." That makes me smile.

"And this is Mrs. Sinelli," Bubbe says. "She took me for a walk yesterday. You're never too old to make new friends, *shayneh maideleh*. Remember that."

"How do you do?" Mrs. Sinelli gives us each a cookie from a box on the coffee table. "My daughter made these herself," Mrs. Sinelli says proudly.

"Thank you," says Bubbe, taking a bite. "Oh, is that good. You have to have something sweet every day, so life won't be bitter." Bubbe wags her finger at me. "Remember that."

After we eat our cookies, we go outside and I sit on a wooden bench next to Bubbe. We watch the sun go down, and then it's time for me to go home. "I'm sad," I say to Bubbe. "I wish I could take you home with me."

Bubbe pats my hand. "I wish you could too, *shayneh maideleh*. But I'm happy we had such a nice time together, and I'll see you next *Shabbos*."

"And the *Shabbos* after that?"

"And the *Shabbos* after that and the *Shabbos* after that," Bubbe answers.

"We had *Shabbos* together when I lived in my apartment, and we had *Shabbos* together when I lived at your house. Now we'll have *Shabbos* together here. Some things change, *shayneh maideleh*," Bubbe says, squeezing my hand, "and some things never change. Remember that."

"I know something that will never change," I say.

"What's that?" Bubbe asks.

"I'll always be your *shayneh maideleh*, and you'll always be my Bubbe."

"That's right," Bubbe says, and now I don't feel so sad anymore.

Before I leave, Bubbe takes some money out of her pocketbook and gives it to me.

"Buy something nice for yourself," she says, "and put some away in the bank. Spend a little and save a little and the rest give away to charity. Even if you have next to nothing," Bubbe says, wagging her finger again, "there's always someone who has less than you. Remember that."

I put the money in my pocket and kiss Bubbe good-bye.

"See you next *Shabbos*," I say.

"Be careful how you cross the street," Bubbe says. "I love you, *shayneh maideleh*. Remember that. Remember everything I tell you, but most of all, remember how much I love you."

"I love you too, Bubbe," I say. I turn around to leave, but then I turn back. "Remember that," I say, shaking my finger the way Bubbe does.

Bubbe laughs and laughs. Then she kisses my face and leaves red lipstick on my cheek, but I don't rub it off until I get all the way home.